Dear Skye

I hope life brings you many
adventures like those in the f...
this book.

Best wishes

*[signature]*

Dar Citron
26. 11. 21

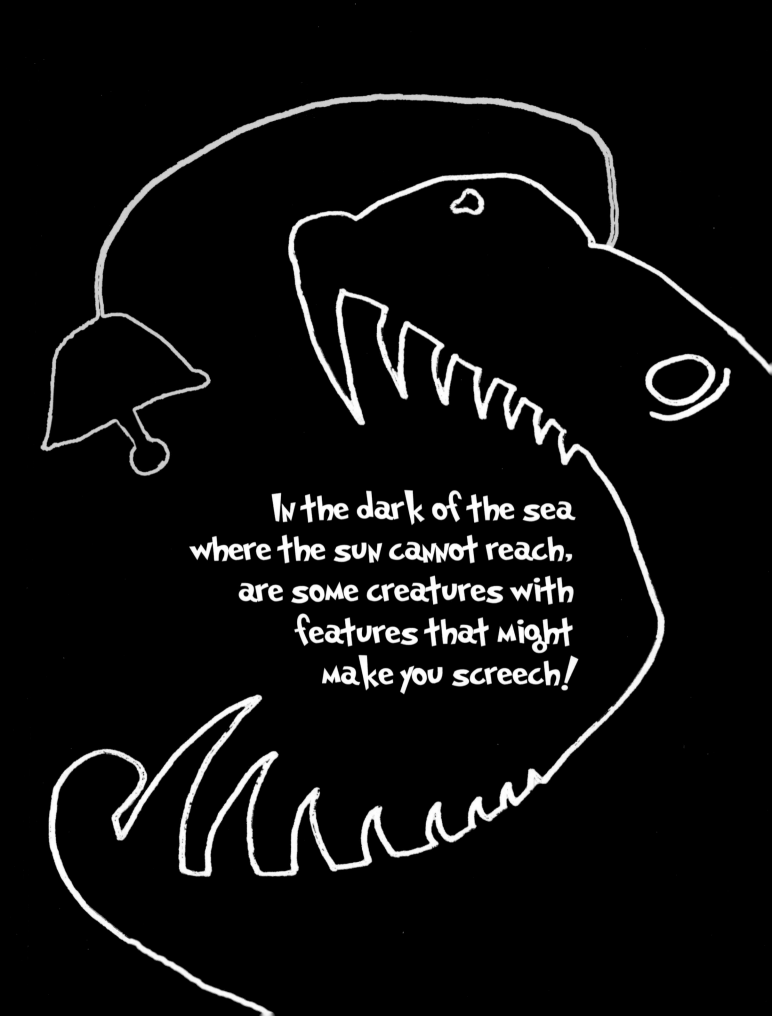

In the dark of the sea
where the sun cannot reach,
are some creatures with
features that might
make you screech!

The blobfish

The angler

The squid and the snail

The fangtooth

The
lanternfish

And the sperm whale

All frolic and play in a world
of their own, deep in the depths
of the dark midnight zone.
You wouldn't find such a
place very nice,
but for cephalopods it
is pure paradise!

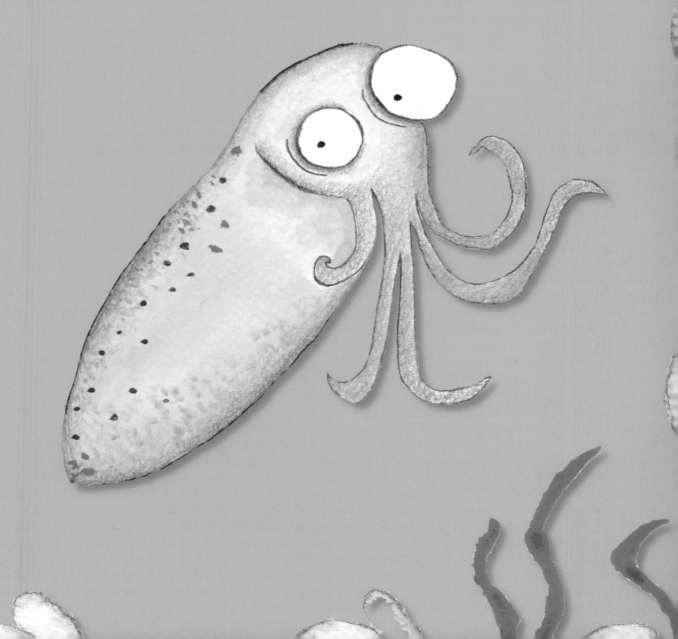

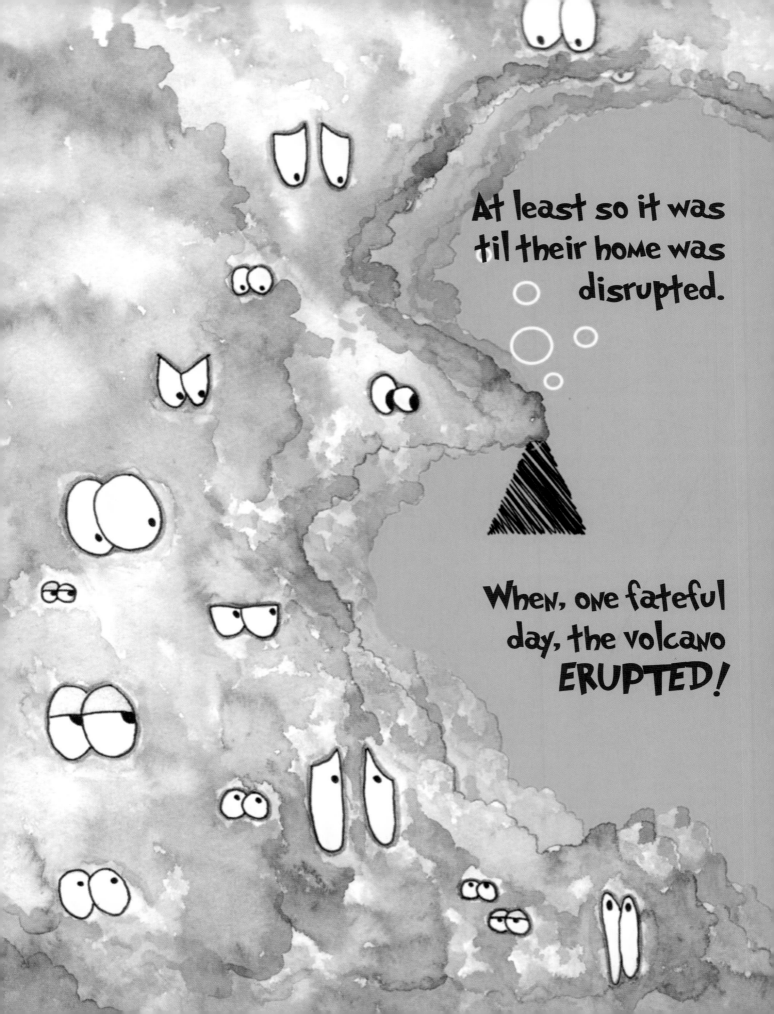

And with this came
changes that none
had foreseen,
deep in this place
where no man had
yet been.

Well, the undersea
creatures made
a start to rebuild.
But it's hard to move
rocks with no hands
and just gills.

Flippers aren't grippers (they all quickly found).
And if you've no bones and just wobble around,

then clearing debris from
a volcanic blast, is
awesome and endless ...

... and hopelessly vast!

The octopus wrapped himself up in a knot, whilst trying to save the blobfish from a spot.

Meanwhile, the angler was trying to free the fangtooth, who'd lost teeth one, two, and three!

When all seemed quite hopeless
the sperm whale announced:

"We cannot live here ... we've all been
de-housed.
It's time we packed up and moved
on our own,
out of the darkness of our midnight zone.
We'll follow the plankton  that lights up the way.
We cannot stay here –

– let's UP and AWAY!"

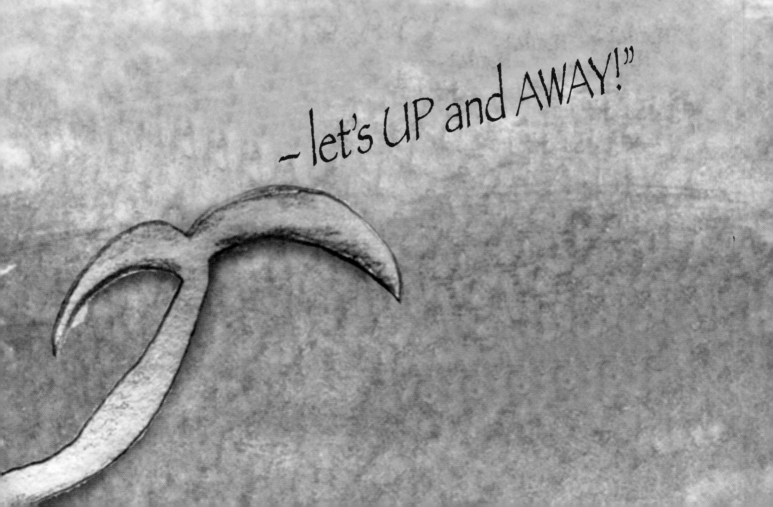

And so they began the most wondrous trail. The fish and the squid, and the tiny sea snail.

All journeyed on upward from their sandy bed.

And none could imagine what might lie ahead.

They travelled together from this place they had known. A place that for so long had been home sweet home.

When they arrived at an old, rusty wreckage, whale told the others:

"Take heed of my message. As you explore this watery maze, don't lose your way in the green salty haze ...

... else you might end up
a suitable nibble for
lobster or shipworm,
for mollusc or gribble.
You'll also find
creatures
who hide in the
shale."

"I hope I'm not eaten by shark!" cried the snail.

An eel slithered by
making sparks as he went.
As he weaved and he curved,
and he doubled and bent.
Molluscs and mussels
gripped tight to the hull,
now rusted and broken,
and faded and dull.

As they were exploring
in each nook and cranny.
They all heard a squeal
very strange and uncanny.
A poor little urchin was
stuck in a spot,
where a girder had fallen
down due to the rot.

Tugging up rusty old metal around, the gang and the others pulled away what they found.

Working with vigour and never a doubt, the gang and the shipwreck crew pulled urchin **OUT!**

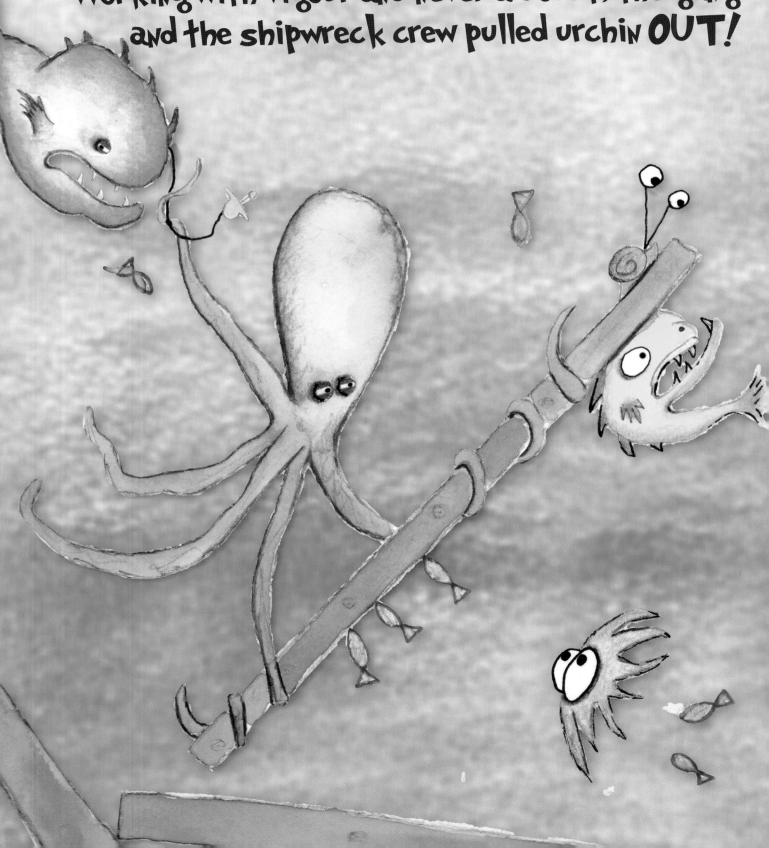

Once all had calmed down the gang looked about.
From bow to the stern, things within and without.
Would this rust bucket, all sunken and tossed,
ever replace the dwelling they'd lost?

All the strange creatures who they had just met
assured them they had no reason to fret.
They'd help them move into this odd rusty shell.
But the gang still agreed they would
soon say 'farewell.'

For a while as they travelled
they felt quite alone,
and then the gang entered
the weird twilight zone.
Here, in this world
the hatchetfish glides,
with mirror-like scales that
play tricks on your eyes.
He hides from his prey
in a hide-and-seek game,
and the gang had to find him
in the deep murky plain.

Jellyfish floated with monster oarfish: could this be the place that would grant them their wish?

Then the hatchetfish spoke (though they knew not from where), and his message was clearer than fresh surface air:

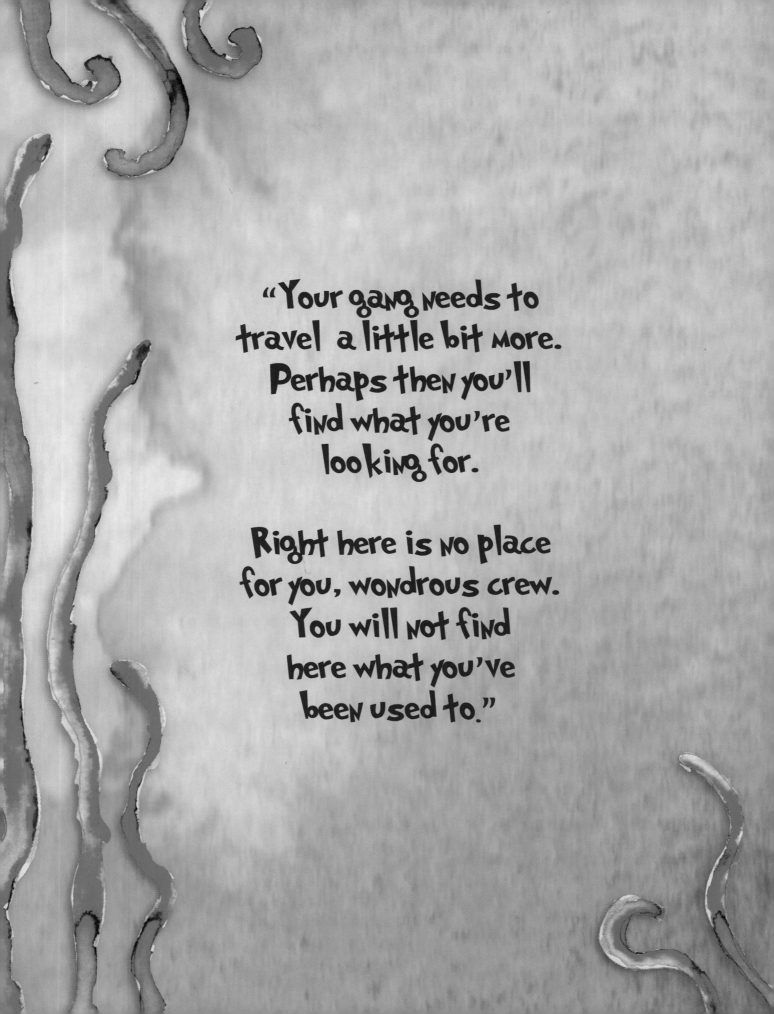

"Your gang needs to
travel a little bit more.
Perhaps then you'll
find what you're
looking for.

Right here is no place
for you, wondrous crew.
You will not find
here what you've
been used to."

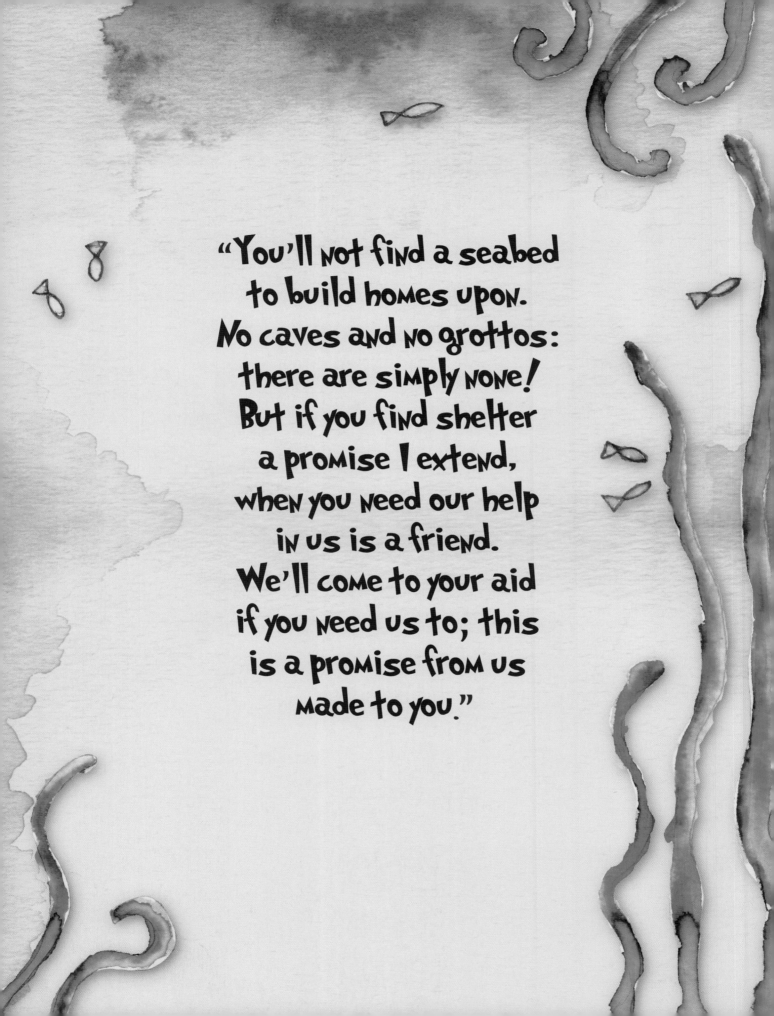

"You'll not find a seabed
to build homes upon.
No caves and no grottos:
there are simply none!
But if you find shelter
a promise I extend,
when you need our help
in us is a friend.
We'll come to your aid
if you need us to; this
is a promise from us
made to you."

So the midnight gang left
still in search of a home.
But for how much longer
would they have to roam?

But had they looked back,
even just for a lark,
they may well have noticed
the loitering SHARK!

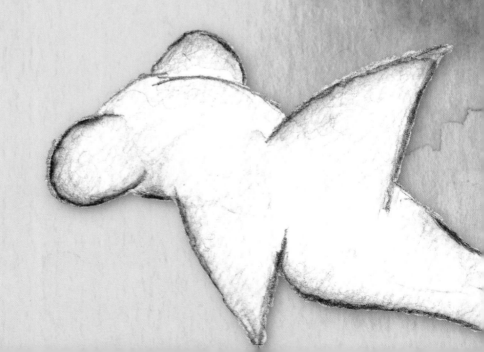

They'd journeyed so far
through the ocean so deep.

Now the midnight zone gang climbed
onto whale for a sleep ...

... and dreamed of a place that they could call theirs.

Finally free from all troubles and cares.

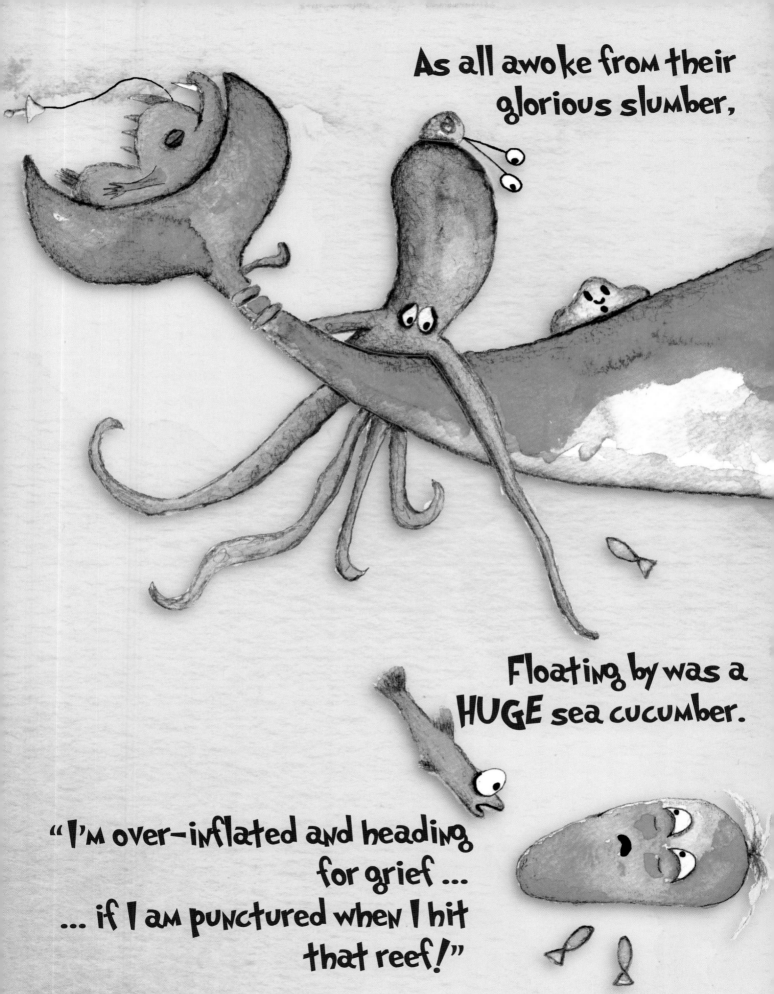

The lanternfish shone as bright as can be.

And, surely enough, the gang could all see ...

... a reef made from coral teeming with life.

"There's no doubt" the snail said "he's heading for strife!"

"Let's make a high wall,"

cried whale loud and gruff.

"if we group where he's heading ...

... he'll just bounce right off!

# "THANKS!"

called cucumber
as he floated away.
The good deed they'd
done him had quite
made their day!

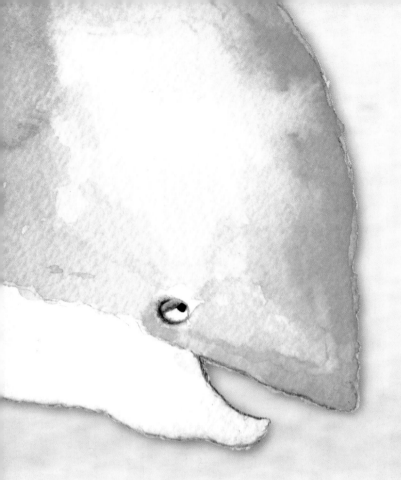

"Cucumber"

**whale told them,**

"has a long way
to go. Right down to
The Trenches
that are lower
than low."

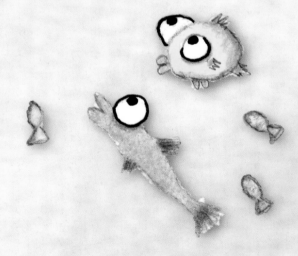

"Our zone is quite deep
where no man can roam.
But far underneath us
Is cucumber's home.

To get there he'll drift
through midnight and more.
Past the abyss to the
vast ocean floor.

We think we've travelled
quite far from our base.
But he's travelled much
further in this distance race."

A pufferfish floating by watching them all, was so scared that he puffed up just like a football!

And all of the creatures who lived in the reef, were laughing and pointing, and giving him grief!

Now, the midnight zone gang
did not like this one bit.
They knew very well
how it felt not to fit.

So the pufferfish joined
them — they'd not laugh
at all, at a fish who
was spiky — and
sometimes a ball!

"No one is perfect;
in fact, we're unique, and
those on the surface have
long legs – and feet!"

"Nothing is stranger,"

**the whale simply said.**

"than a human,
who has lots of hair
on their head."

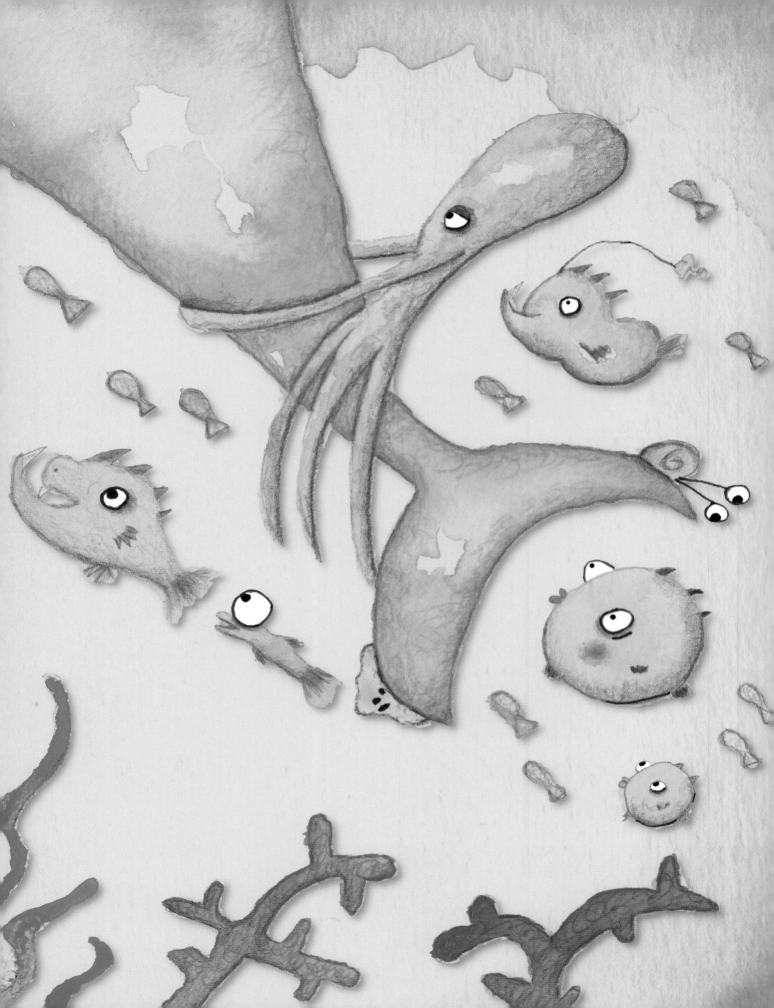

And so they swam over the beautiful reef,
with seahorses and sponges, and
turtles beneath. Now hidden
away in the shadowy dark,
patiently watching,
was that mighty
SHARK!

The hubbub of noise from the back had been growing, and something quite new with the gang was worth knowing.

That as they departed a place every time, other creatures and fish would tag onto their line.

And what had been only a small group of ten ...

... had grown so much now there were hundreds of them!

All searching as one for
adventure to share,
and hoping that they all
could settle somewhere.

They'd journeyed, by now,
many nautical miles, from
seabeds and shipwrecks,
to coral reef isles.

They'd swum through the
midnight, the twilight,
and more, and made many
friends — plus had fans
by the score.

But even the smallest fish had
to bemoan, that the midnight
zone gang still did not
have a home.

Throughout their long trip, every hour or so, the sperm whale would surface (he had to, you know).

To take in some air from the world up above. Then return to the friends who he cared for and loved.

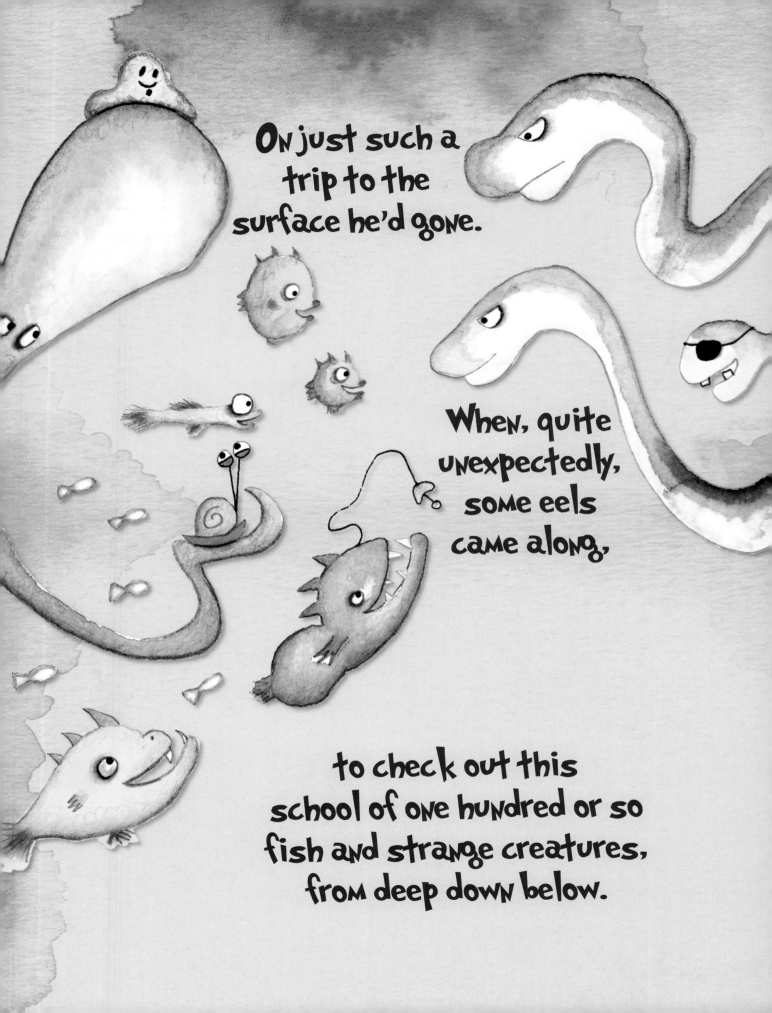

But the eels were not looking to make a new friend. Those slippery creatures, who wriggle and bend, were having great fun with the midnight zone team ...

... by bumping and bashing them, letting off steam.

Their bullying tactics were causing much worry. And all were now wishing for whale — in a hurry!

Then, out of the shadows, the gloom
and the dark, streaking towards
them was the mighty SHARK!

"Oh no!" cried the snail.
"We're shark food for sure!"

But none had expected
what next lay in
store ...

The shark
hadn't come
to eat all the
fish (though
for sure they
would make
a nice tasty
dish).

Not to munch
them and crunch
them, those
yummy fish
meals ...

He'd watched from afar as the crew searched the sea, from shipwreck to coral, intrigued massively. Shark had been searching in life for a place where he'd be accepted, and not a disgrace. A shark who is friendly is a hard thing to prove, but now was his chance to make this his move. To show beyond doubt that things weren't as they seemed, and not EVERY shark is scary and mean.

When the eels saw the
shark it was too late to run.
And they knew that
this meeting would
not be much fun.

With one mighty shove
the eels' game was ended.
A glint of shark's teeth
had them tossed
and up-ended!

As they splashed and they scrambled
to get out of shark's path, a flip
from his tail nearly split them in half!
The splashing and thrashing turned
calm sea to foam.
Then, thanks to the shark,
the eels were soon gone.

The gang cheered the shark
with a mighty HOORAY!
for being a hero
and saving the day.

Our whale soon arrived
to check out the commotion,
but greeting him was
a calm, settled ocean.

The gang had been saved
from those eels who could bend ...

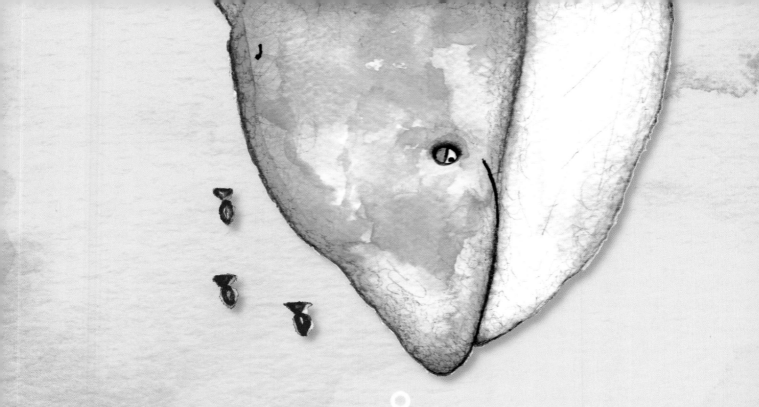

... and now in their group was a shark — and a friend.

All were elated with eels now long gone.

So whale took the lead and the search carried on.

Puffer fish, chatting to fangtooth that night, asked him:

"Why do we follow whale; why is that right?
Is it because he's so big and so brave?"

Well, this is the answer the fangtooth fish gave ...

"Whale is the kindest, most caring of creatures. His heart is so big that his love never peters.

That's why we trust our great whale so much so. Because love is the greatest of gifts that we know."

Just then whale
announced:

"We've been getting this
wrong! Midnight is where
we all truly belong."

"If we head way back down
to that deepest dark zone,
I have a good feeling
we'll not be alone,
So, trust me again as
you have done before.
And I'll show you something
you'll like, I feel sure."

Those who had travelled so far and so long, had
made many friends as they'd journeyed on.

So, when they returned to their dark, salty lair,
all the friends they had made were
with them right there.

And now, with their help and no longer alone,
they rebuilt their world in the deep midnight zone.

It all came to pass that with
friends, love and laughter.
They thrived and they grew
to live happily ever after.

They'd been right in their
choice to get behind whale.
To trust him and follow
his whopping great tail.

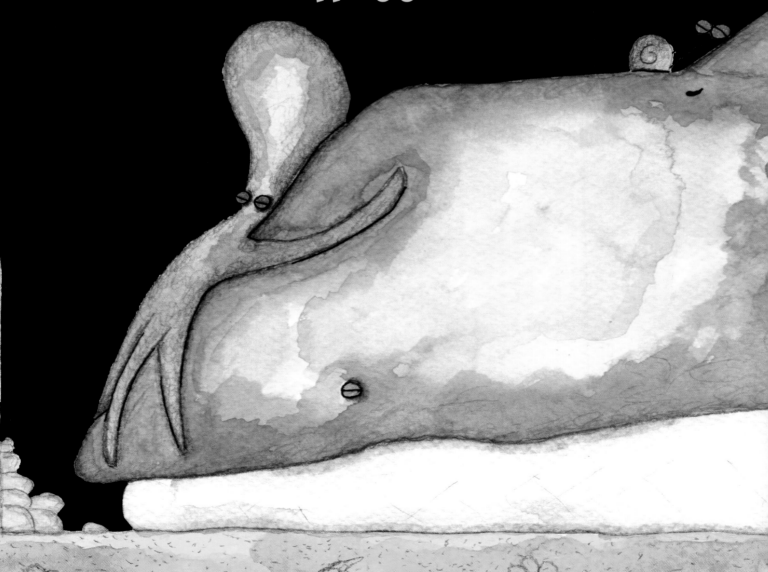

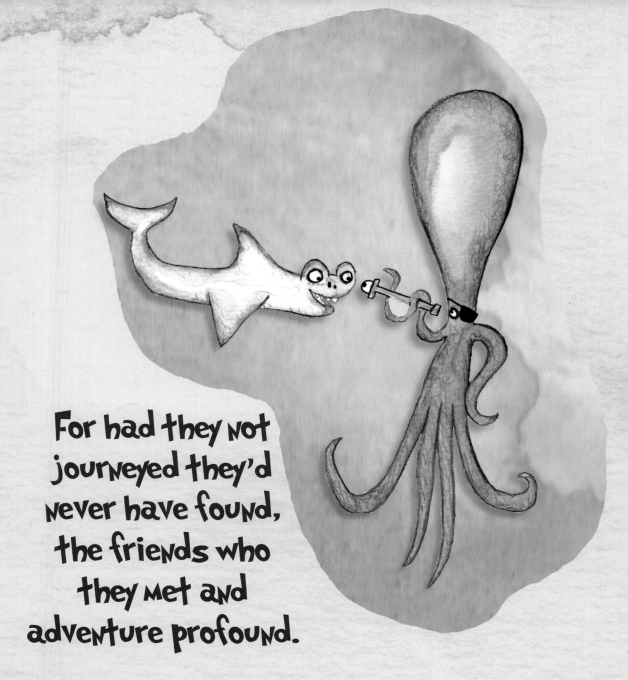

For had they not
journeyed they'd
never have found,
the friends who
they met and
adventure profound.

And they'd never have
learned that the ship
which is best,
is friendship, that's
stronger than all of
the rest!

The
End

The Hubble & Hattie imprint was launched in 2009, and is named in memory of two very special Westie sisters owned by Veloce's proprietors. Since the first book, many more have been added, all with the same objective: to be of real benefit to the species they cover; at the same time promoting compassion, understanding and respect between all animals (including human ones!)

Our new range of books for kids will champion the same values and standards that we've always held dear, but to the adults of the future. Children will love reading, or have read to them, these beautifully illustrated, carefully crafted publications, absorbing valuable life lessons whilst being highly entertained.

We've more great books already in the pipeline so be sure to check out our website for details.

## Other great books from our Hubble & Hattie Kids! imprint

9781787111608

9781787112926

9781787115156

9781787113077

9781787113862

9781787115163

9781787113060

9781787117198

9781787114180

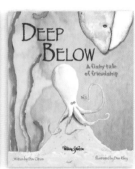
9781787117464

9781787116993

9781787113121

9781787117389

9781787114302

9781787117372

# www.hubbleandhattie.com

First published October 2021 by Veloce Publishing Limited, Veloce House, Parkway Farm Business Park, Middle Farm Way, Poundbury, Dorchester, Dorset, DT1 3AR, England. Tel 01305 260068/Fax 01305 250479/email info@hubbleandhattie.com/web www.hubbleandhattie.com
ISBN: 978-1-787117-46-4 UPC: 6-36847-01746-0 ©Dov Citron, Dee Riley & Veloce Publishing Ltd 2021. All rights reserved. With the exception of quoting brief passages for the purpose of review, no part of this publication may be recorded, reproduced or transmitted by any means, including photocopying, without the written permission of Veloce Publishing Ltd. Throughout this book logos, model names and designations, etc, have been used for the purposes of identification, illustration and decoration. Such names are the property of the trademark holder as this is not an official publication. Readers with ideas for books about animals, or animal-related topics, are invited to write to the publisher of Veloce Publishing at the above address. British Library Cataloguing in Publication Data – A catalogue record for this book is available from the British Library. Typesetting, design and page make-up all by Veloce Publishing Ltd on Apple Mac. Printed in India by Parksons Graphics.